Usborne
Wipe-Clean
Construction Site
Activities

Illustrated by Gareth Williams
Designed by Laura Hammonds
Written by Kirsteen Robson

Use your wipe-clean pen to do all the
activities in this fun-filled book.

6   7   8   9   10

Starting to build

Follow the lines to see who is holding the other end of Daisy's measuring tape.

Rowan

Rocco

Daisy

Count the bricks in each pile. Then, trace over the numbers.

6   3   5

Connect the dots to finish the concrete mixer truck.

Spot 5 differences between these two mini dump trucks.

New homes

Use the pen to show Don the way to the house where Kyle is waiting for a delivery.

Don

Draw over the dots to finish these three new houses.

Find and circle 4 wheelbarrows.

Kyle

Write an X under the front loader that does not match the others.

Building houses

Draw over the dots to finish the roof and windows.

Draw 5 more rungs to finish the ladder.

Draw 6 more bricks on Barry's wall.

Barry

Spot 5 differences between the two houses below.

Connect the dots to finish the truck.

On the inside

Find and circle 7 pencils.

Draw over the dots to see where Cyril will paint.

Cyril

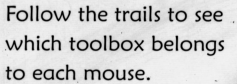

Follow the trails to see which toolbox belongs to each mouse.

Circle the shape that does not have one to match it.

Draw lines to match the paint rollers to the cans of paint.

Baz

Trace the lines to show Baz where to lay the floor tiles.

Digging up the road

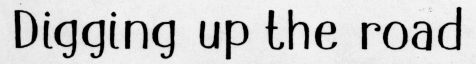

Draw 2 wheels on all the cars that need them.

Kit

Use the pen to show Kit and the road roller the way to Casey's patch of road.

Draw over the dots to finish the pipes.

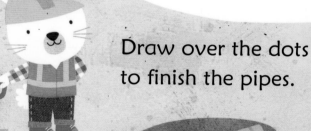

2 3 4

Count the yellow stripes on the three barriers above, then trace over the numbers.

Casey

Draw around the piece of pipe that Kat needs to connect the pipes below.

Kat

Building a playground

Connect each set of dots to finish the play equipment.

Draw 2 more post holes that Kat and Rocco have made with their auger.

Kat

Rocco

Find and circle 5 pigeons.

Draw over the dots to finish the swings.

Follow the trails to see which mouse will pick up more bolts on the way to Sandy.

Sandy

Building high

Draw over the dots to finish the skyscrapers.

Spot 4 differences between these two tower cranes.

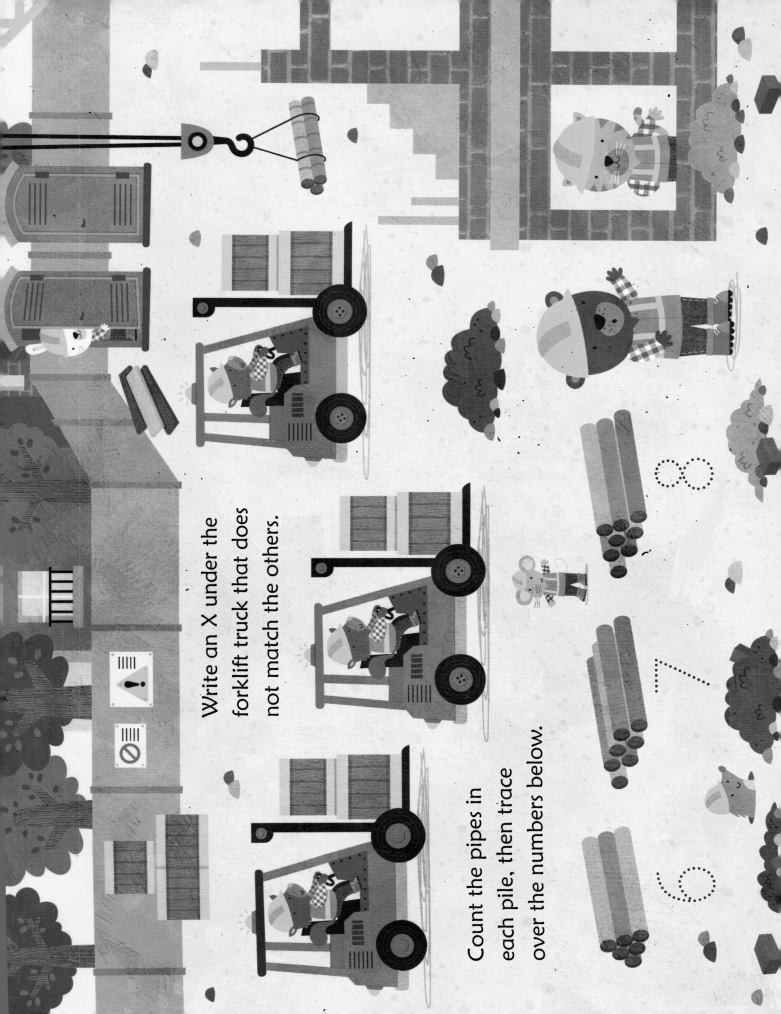

Write an X under the forklift truck that does not match the others.

Count the pipes in each pile, then trace over the numbers below.

In the city

Write an X under the car that does not match any other.

Connect the dots to finish the site office.

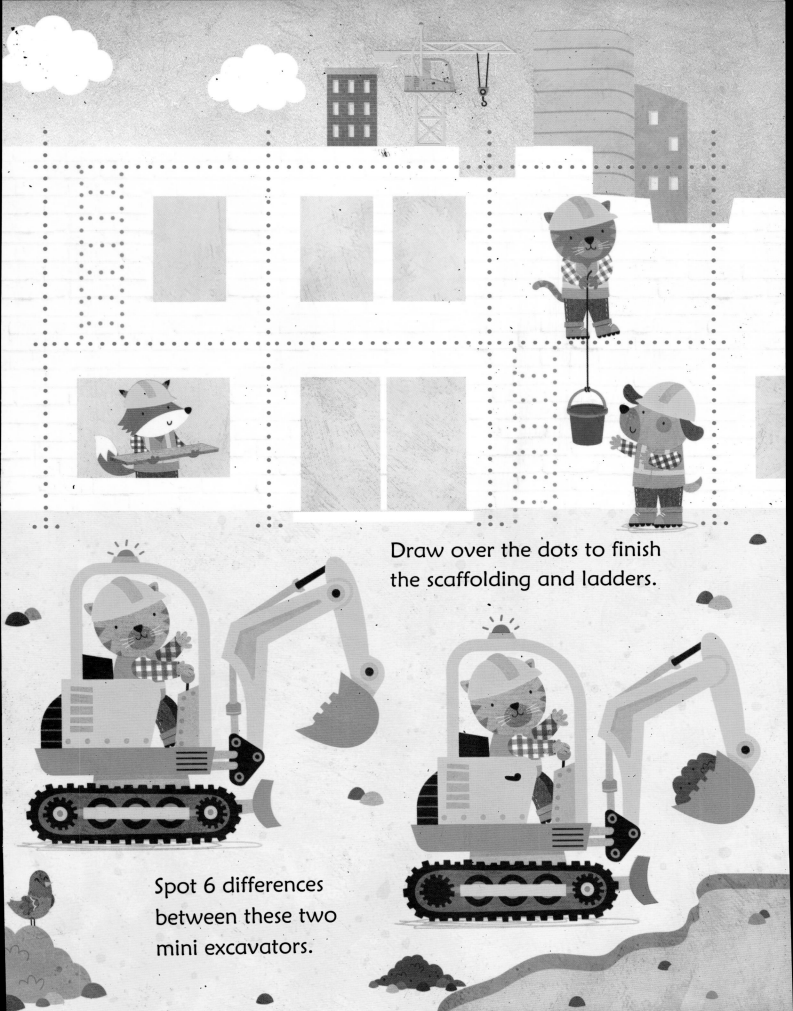

Draw over the dots to finish the scaffolding and ladders.

Spot 6 differences between these two mini excavators.

Bridge builders

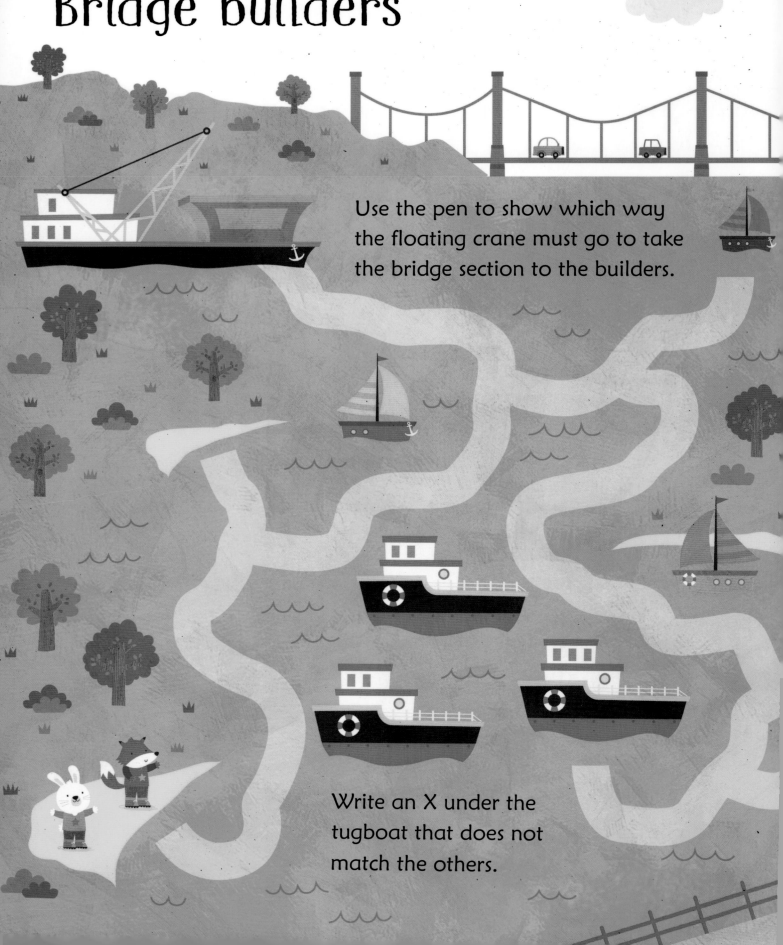

Use the pen to show which way the floating crane must go to take the bridge section to the builders.

Write an X under the tugboat that does not match the others.

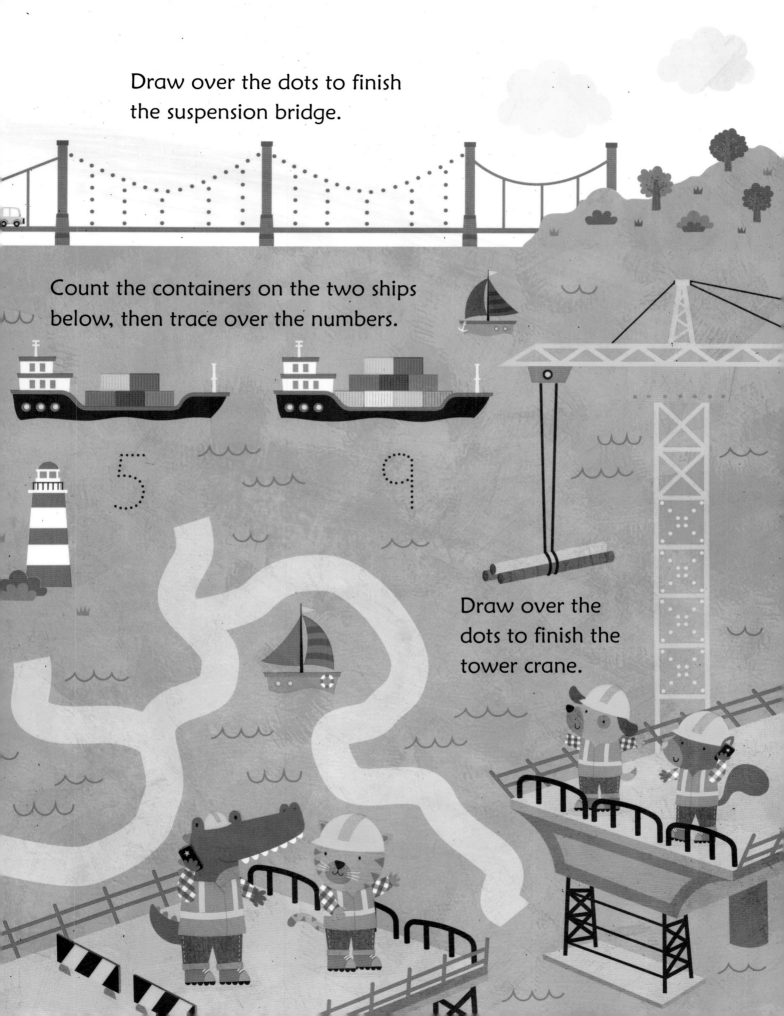

Draw over the dots to finish
the suspension bridge.

Count the containers on the two ships
below, then trace over the numbers.

5

9

Draw over the
dots to finish the
tower crane.

Demolition site

Spot 7 differences between these two heavy load dump trucks.

Follow the trails to see whose wheelbarrow is whose.